ST. JAMES'S HALL,

REGENT STREET AND PICCADILLY.

MONDAY

POPULAR CONCERTS.

Programmes and Analytical Remarks.

SEVENTEENTH SEASON.

1874-75.

PRICE FIFTEEN SHILLINGS.

J. MALLETT, PRINTER, 59, WARDOUR STREET, SOHO, LONDON. W.

Monday Popular Concerts,

SEVENTEENTH SEASON, 1874-5.

DIRECTOR—Mr. S. ARTHUR CHAPPELL.

THE Director begs to announce that the Seventeenth Season of the Monday Popular Concerts commences on Monday Evening, November 9, and that the Performances will take place as follows, viz:—

MONDAY, NOVEMBER 9, 1874.	MONDAY, JANUARY 25, 1875.
,, ,, 16.	,, FEBRUARY 1.
,, ,, 23.	,, ,, 8.
,, ,, 30.	,, ,, 15.
,, DECEMBER 7.	,, ,, 22.
,, ,, 14.	,, MARCH 1.
,, JANUARY 11, 1875.	,, ,, 8.
,, ,, 18.	,, ,, 15.

The Director's Benefit takes place on Monday, March 22nd.

Sixteen Morning Performances will be given on Saturdays, November 14, 21, 28, December 5, 12, and 19, 1874; January 16, 23, 30, February 6, 13, 20, 27, March 6, 13, and 20, 1875.

For the accommodation of those who may desire to occupy the same seats at every performance, the Director will continue to issue Subscription Tickets, at £3 10s. (transferable), entitling holders to special Sofa Stalls, selected by

B

themselves, for the whole Series of 16 Monday Evening Concerts, extending from Monday, Nov. 9, to March 15.

Subscription Tickets are also issued for the 16 Morning Concerts, at £3 10s. extending from Saturday Afternoon, Nov. 14, to March 20; also for the 7 Morning Concerts, taking place on Saturdays, January 16, 23, 30, February 6, 13, 20, and 27, at £1 10s.

Dr. HANS VON BÜLOW will appear on Mondays, November 9, 16, and 30; also on Saturdays, November 14, 21, and December 19.

Miss AGNES ZIMMERMANN will be the Pianist on Monday Evening, November 23; and on Saturday Afternoon, November 28.

Mr. CHARLES HALLÉ will appear on Monday, December 7, and on Saturday, December 5.

Madame NORMAN-NÉRUDA will be the Violinist on Mondays, November 23, December 7 and 14; also on Saturdays, November 28, December 5 and 12.

M. SAINTON is engaged for Monday Evening, November 9, and Saturday Afternoon, November 14.

Herr STRAUS will lead on Monday Evenings, November 16 and 30.

Signor PIATTI will hold the post of First Violoncello on all occasions after the Concerts of November 9 and 14; Herr L. RIES, that of Second Violin; Herr STRAUS or Mr. ZERBINI will play Viola; Sir JULIUS BENEDICT and Mr. ZERBINI, as heretofore, officiating as Conductors.

Mr. SIMS REEVES is engaged on Monday Evening, December 7; and Mr. SANTLEY will appear on Monday Evening, November 23, and on Saturdays, November 28 and December 12.

Madlle. MARIE KREBS, Herr DANNREUTHER, Mr. FRANKLIN TAYLOR, and Herr JOACHIM, will appear after Christmas.

MONDAY POPULAR CONCERTS.

MONDAY EVENING, NOVEMBER 9th, 1874.

PROGRAMME.

PART I.

QUARTET, in E flat, Op. 44, No. 3, for two Violins,
Viola, and Violoncello.................................*Mendelssohn.*

MM. SAINTON, L. RIES, ZERBINI, and PEZZE.

LIEDER, " Dichterliebe," Nos. 1, 2, 7, and 8................. *Schumann.*

Miss ANTOINETTE STERLING.

SONATA, in E major, Op. 109, for Pianoforte alone ......*Beethoven.*

Dr. HANS VON BÜLOW.

PART II.

SONATA, in A major, Op. 69, for Pianoforte and
Violoncello ....*Beethoven.*

Dr. HANS VON BÜLOW and Signor PEZZE.

NEW SONG, "Thou art weary."................. ....*Arthur Sullivan.*

Miss ANTOINETTE STERLING.

TRIO, in B flat, Op. 52, for Pianoforte, Violin, and
Violoncello..*Rubinstein.*

MM. HANS VON BÜLOW, SAINTON, and PEZZE.

Conductor   -   Sir JULIUS BENEDICT.

The Director regrets to announce that Signor PIATTI is prevented by indisposition from appearing this Evening, but hopes to make his first appearance this Season on Monday next, November 16th.
November 9th, 1874.

Monday Popular Concerts.

——

DIRECTOR—Mr. S. ARTHUR CHAPPELL.

Four Hundred and Eighty-sixth Concert.*

PROGRAMME FROM THE WORKS OF

Various Masters.

MONDAY EVENING, NOVEMBER 9th, 1874.

* First Concert of the Seventeenth Season.

QUARTET, in E flat major, Op. 44, No. 3, for two Violins, Viola, and Violoncello. *Mendelssohn.*

(Thirteenth performance at the Popular Concerts.)

Allegro vivace—E flat major.
Scherzo, assai leggiere e vivace—C minor.
Adagio non troppo—A flat major.
Molto allegro con fuoco—E flat major.

M. SAINTON, Herr L. RIES, Mr. ZERBINI,
and Signor PEZZE.

The three quartets, Op. 44, are to Mendelssohn what the Rasoumoffsky quartets are to Beethoven. They were produced in the maturity of his talent, and, besides being masterpieces of ingenious construction, are among the happiest productions of his inventive genius. The one now introduced is the last of the set. Its *scherzo* alone would stamp it as exclusively the work of Mendelssohn ; for no other composer (Beethoven— whose *scherzi* differ essentially from those of Mendelssohn— not excepted) has written anything of the kind. But though this may be the movement most characteristic of its author's individual idiosyncracy, its three companions are equally successful, and have equal shares in a whole which has every right to be considered a *chef-d'œuvre*. The first *allegro*, thus vigorously announced :—

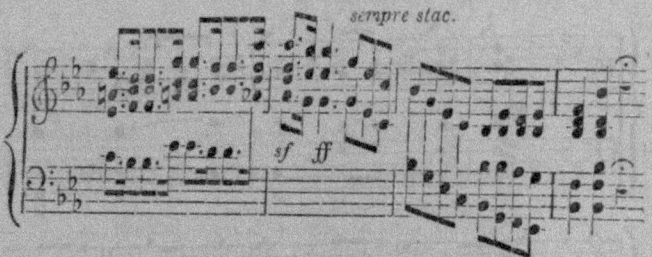

—has hardly a superior for variety and interest of contrivance, to say nothing of its abundant melody, and the admirable skill with which its themes are made to contrast with and relieve each other. The *scherzo*, to which allusion has been made, will be recognised at once by the opening theme :—

The plan of this movement is as regular and well defined as that of the *allegro*, although it is naturally more concise

and epigrammatic in development. The quaint second subject
—first appearing in G minor :—

—and the fairy-like *fughetta*, which constitutes the most
remarkable episode—the theme given out by the viola :—

—are true inspirations; and perhaps a more notable example of fancy and scholarship going hand in hand than the latter does not exist in music. The third movement, *adagio* (in A flat), but that the Mendelssohnian colouring is apparent from beginning to end, might have been composed by Mozart, so unceasing and enchanting is its melody:—

The conduct of this admirable movement, and the thorough completeness with which the themes are wrought out, proclaim a master yielding to none in the highest qualifications that warrant the name. The *finale*, beginning thus:—

—one of those rapid, vehement, and agitated "*prestos*" of which Mendelssohn has left so many perfect examples—is a worthy ending to a composition which, in the domain of chamber music, according to modern feeling, Beethoven alone can be said to have surpassed.

The Quartet in E flat was first introduced by Herr Becker, Herr L. Ries, Mr. Doyle, and Signor Piatti, at the eighth concert of the second season—January 16th, 1860.

LIEDER, Miss ANTOINETTE STERLING.

Schumann.

"IM WUNDERSCHÖNEN MONAT MAI."

Im wunderschönen Monat Mai,
　Als alle Knospen sprangen,
Da ist in meinem Herzen
　Die Liebe aufgegangen.

Im wunderschönen Monat Mai,
　Als alle Vögel sangen,
Da hab' ich ihr gestanden
　Mein Sehnen und Verlangen.

A MAY SONG.

'Twas in the lovely month of May,
　And all the buds were springing,
My heart it felt so light and gay,
　And love's first song was singing.

'Twas in the lovely month of May,
　When birds were warbling cheerly,
'Twas then I to my love did say,
　"I love thee, ah! how dearly!"

"AUS MEINEN THRÄNEN SPRIESSEN."

Aus meinen Thränen spriessen
　Viel blühende Blumen hervor,
Und meine Seufzer werden
　Ein Nachtigallenchor;
Und wenn du, mich Lieb, hast Kindchen,
　Schenk' ich dir die Blumen all',
Und vor deinem Fenster soll klingen
　Das Lied der Nachtigall.

LOVE'S TEARS.

Where'er my tears are falling,
　There bloom the brightest flow'rs;
My sighs, like nightingales warbling,
　Seem echoing 'mid the bow'rs;
And when thou shalt love me, dearest,
　Fairest blossoms shall be thine;
And the nightingales 'neath thy window
　Shall sing when thou art mine.

"ICH GROLLE NICHT."

Ich grolle nicht und wenn das Herz auch bricht,
Ewig verlornes Lieb!
Wie du auch strahlst in Diamentenpracht,
Es fällt kein Strahl in deines Herzens Nacht,
Das weiss ich längst.

Ich grolle nicht und wenn das Herz auch bricht.
Ich sah dich ja im Traume,
Und sah die Nacht in deines Herzens Raume,
Und sah die Schlang', die dir am Herzen frisst—
Ich sah mein Lieb, wie sehr du elend bist.
Ich grolle nicht.

"I WILL NOT GRIEVE."

I will not grieve, although my heart should break,
Though thou art lost to me—
Though thou couldst thus deceive!
Though diamonds deck, and boundless wealth be thine,
No ray of joy upon thy heart shall shine;
Nor will I grieve!

I will not grieve, although my heart should break!
I dreamt it long ago,
That thou wouldst cause me cruel grief and woe.
I've seen the serpent on my heart that preys,
And known thy hapless hours and weary days.
I will not grieve!

"UND WÜSSTEN'S DIE BLUMEN."

Und wüssten's die Blumen die kleinen
  Wie tief verwundet mein Herz,
Sie würden mit mir weinen,
  Zu heilen meinen Schmerz.

Und wüssten's die Nachtigallen
  Wie ich so traurig und krank,
Sie liesen fröhlich erschallen
  Erquickenden Gesang.

Und wüssten sie mein Wehe,
  Die goldenen Sternelein,
Sie kämen aus ihrer Höhe,
  Und sprächen Trost mir ein.

Sie alle können's nicht wissen,
  Nur Eine kennt meinen Schmerz;
Sie hat ja selbst zerrissen,
  Zerrissen mir das Herz.

GRIEF.

If the flow'rets so fair only knew
  How deep my bosom's pain,
They'd shed for me their tears of dew,
  Like sweet refreshing rain.

And if the nightingales
  But knew how sad am I,
They'd breathe their sweetest tales,
  In blithesome melody.

And if my grief were known
  To the stars that through ether roll,
Each one would descend from his throne,
  And whisper hope to my soul.

By spirits ne'er 'twill be known—
  Only one my pain can guess;
And she, the cause, alone
  Can know my heart's distress.

Nos. 1, 2, 7, and 8, of a collection of Songs, by Robert Schumann, entitled *Dichterliebe* (Poet's Love). The English words are by X. M. Hayes.

———

SONATA, in E major, Op. 109, for Pianoforte alone.* *Beethoven.*

(Fourth performance at the Popular Concerts.)

Vivace ma non troppo⎱
Adagio espressivo ......⎰
Tempo primo .... ⎬—E major.
Adagio espressivo ......⎰
Tempo primo ....⎭
Prestissimo—E minor.
Andante molto cantabile; theme with variations — No. 1,
    Molto espressivo—No. 2, Leggieramente—No. 3, Allegro
    vivace—No. 4, Un poco andante—No. 5, Allegro ma non
    troppo (fugue)—No. 6, Tempo del tema, cantabile;—E
    major.

Dr. HANS VON BÜLOW.

Beethoven published no work of importance between the great sonata in B flat, Op. 106, and the three last pianoforte sonatas, Nos. 109, 110, and 111. The Op. 109, in E, and 110, in A flat, were both composed in 1821, while the great master was busily engaged with his *Missa Solenentis*, No. 2 (in D major).

If in the sonata, Op. 106—in which Beethoven appears to have solaced himself almost exclusively with the intellectual exhibition of his art, in the E major sonata, Op. 109, we find the great musician once more a poet, once more depressed, once more in love with an ideal. It little matters who or what was Mlle. Maximiliana Brentano, to whom this romantic and beautiful work is dedicated; whether she was the celebrated "Bettina," afterwards Frau von Arnim, who raved about Beethoven in her letters to Goethe, and to whom Beethoven is said to have first played over his "Kennst du das Land?"—or whether she was that lady's sister, also a Brentano of Frankfort-on-the-Main. Perhaps the young lady was only another shadow of that ideal which Beethoven had conceived, and which "Bettina" and others had been unable to realise. To these dreams we are indebted for poems out of number; and among them there is, perhaps, not one that exceeds in beauty the pianoforte sonata in E major, Op. 109—between which, and the Op. 101, the colossal "B flat" (Op. 106) is the connecting link. The very opening discloses a reaction in the mind of Beethoven. His old feeling has come back. He is irresolute and unhappy; and this state is clearly mirrored in his harmonious inspiration. The sonata begins furtively, as though

* No. 31 of Beethoven's Sonatas, edited by Mr. CHARLES HALLÉ —published by Chappell and Co. 50, New Bond Street.

the master had not made up his mind as to what he was about to say :—

The sudden interruption of the foregoing, by a mysterious *adagio :*—

—which, after a few irregular measures, including an appropriate *cadenza*, gives way to a long and extremely interesting development of the leading theme, again supplants it, and again retires, to allow of its being fully wrought out—reveals in a strong light the irresolution under which the composer was temporarily labouring. The first theme is resumed in a modified shape :—

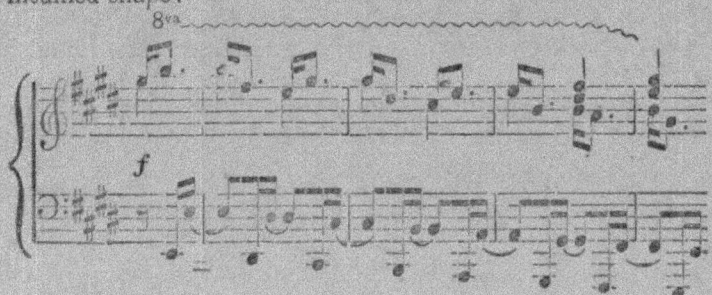

The second apparition of the *adagio espressivo*—now expected in E, as it was previously expected in B, but commencing as before on a discord:—

is followed by a still more brilliant *cadenza*, at the termination of which, after a *ritardando*, the leading theme steals gently back on a new division of the scale as though about to develop itself in another key (A)—an illusion which is dissipated at the end of the second bar:—

The predominant character of this very original movement is a mixture of languor and aspiration, which seem to arrest each other by fits and starts. A dozen points might be quoted; but one more only—the beauty of which will strike every attentive hearer—must suffice:—

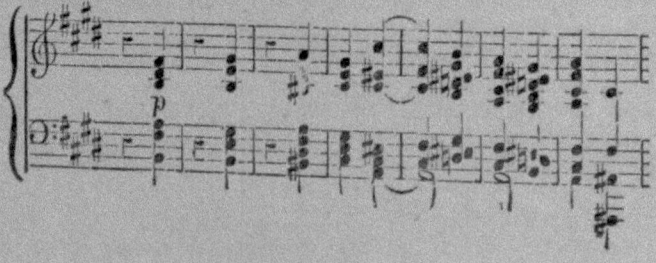

With the working out of this, through a very few bars—
the melody gradually ascending, "*pianissimo*," to the higher
regions of the key-board—the first movement, which appears
rather to evaporate than to end, is achieved. That Beethoven's
spirit, once more in fetters, has thrown aside all the disdain
so energetically uttered, and with such elaborate expression,
in the Fugue (*allegro risoluto*) of "Op. 106," is manifest.
Wrapped in an atmosphere of dreams, the master resigns
himself to their control. At the end of the *vivace ma non
troppo* ("*vivace*" is a singular epithet to apply to such a
train of thought), one might fancy him slumbering; but how
suddenly he awakes from his trance, and with what vigour
he shakes off the trammels to which he has unconsciously
submitted, appears in the impetuous outset of the next movement (*prestissimo*—E minor):—

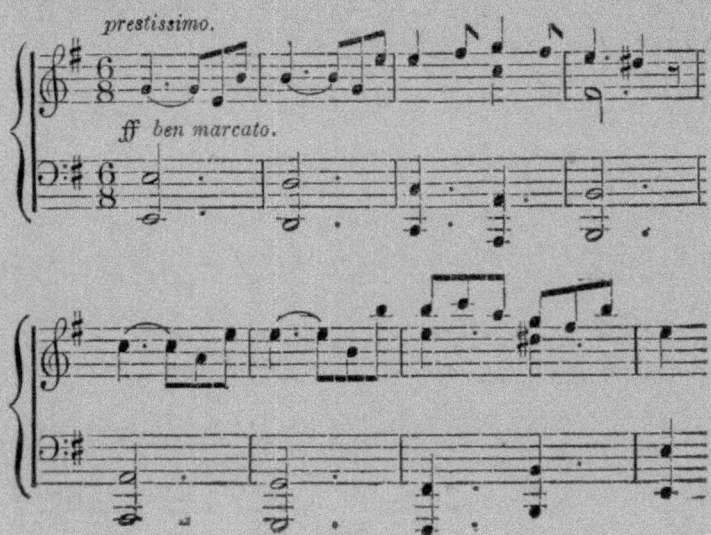

The continuation—on a dominant *pedale*—though marked *piano*, is of a no less agitated character :—

This, after a full close in E minor, gives place to a new subject in the same key, entering in unison :—

—which, briefly developed, is followed by the introduction to the second subject—also on a dominant *pedale* (B), and bearing a strong affinity to the continuation of the leading theme (quoted above) :—

The vehemently agitated character of the preceding is in some degree relieved by the softer and gentler, though by no means more cheerful, melody of the second subject proper, which comes in upon a discord :—

and comprises the subjoined beautiful episode, in transition :—

This without attaining a full close in C major, affords the composer an opportunity for a delicate employment of his favorite device, in resorting to the minor second of the key :—

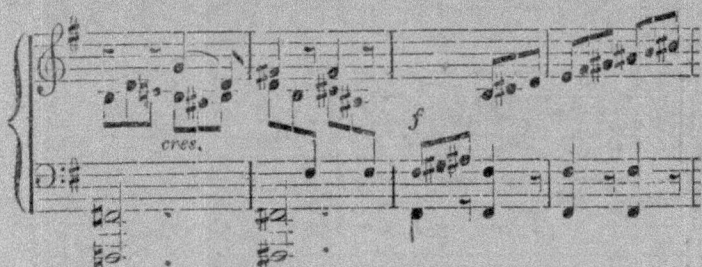

A vigorous passage in strict double counterpoint, which grows out of the foregoing, brings this section of the movement to a close, in the dominant minor (B); upon which an interesting episode ensues, introduced upon a *pedale* :—

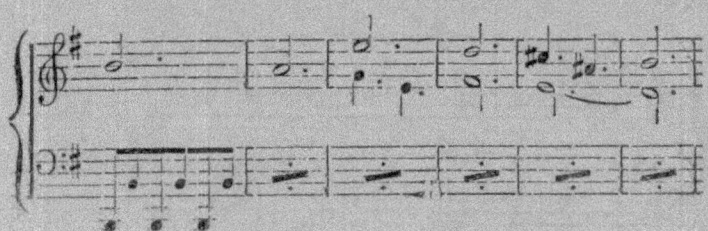

When at length the *pedale* has resolved itself into the key of C, we have a wonderful development of this episode, which brings us eventually to the dominant of the dominant (F sharp) —or, as it may be easier understood, the supertonic of the original key of E minor:—

At the point where the *coda* is arrested (four bars before the end of the above quotation), Beethoven would seem again to have relapsed intto a trance ; but rousing himself by a strong effort of volition, he resumes his leading theme with a sudden impetuosity.   The re-appearance of this in the key of E minor, directly after the close in F sharp major (see * in the foregoing example) is one of those independent strokes of genius that startle and interest, while they impress the hearer. Beethoven's works are full of them ; but a bolder instance could hardly be cited.   The theme on repetition is now put to the test of free double-counterpoint :—

Former bass, modified.

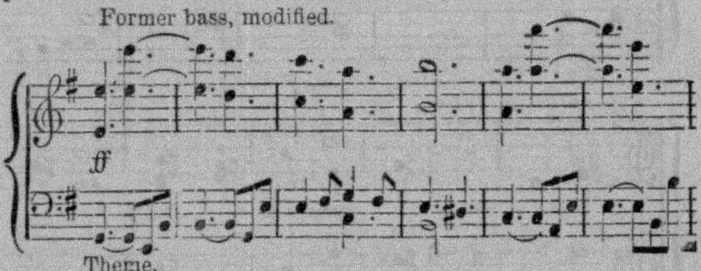

Theme.

A recapitulation of the first part now succeeds in appropriate keys; and the *Prestissimo* is brought to a conclusion with the following brief and characteristic *coda* :—

The plan of this *Scherzo* is precisely that of a first movement.   From a state of mental hesitation Beethoven now at length emerges, to imagine one of the most exquisite of those original melodies which he has treated in the "variation" form.   Thus does the *Andante molto cantabile* (E major) commence :—

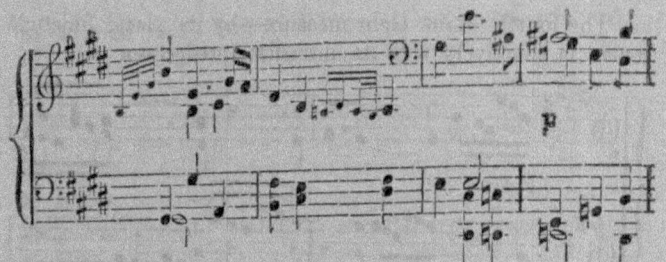

The first and simplest variation—in the same measure as the theme—begins as subjoined (the melody will suffice) :—

The second—also in the measure of the theme, and one of the most fanciful of the series—as subjoined :—

This comprises an episode of a highly expressive character :—

The third variation—in two-four measure—is of a more eccentric turn :—

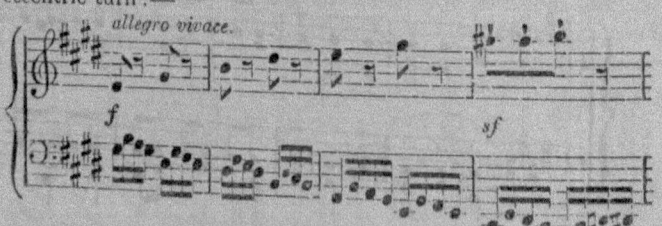

The fourth—nine-eight measure—by its placid quietude contrasts effectively with its immediate predecessor :—

The fifth variation—common-time—begins thus :—

is continued thus :—

and developed throughout, with masterly skill, in the fugued style. A single quotation from the sixth variation—the longest, and most interesting of all—would afford but an imperfect idea of the ingenious variety of its treatment. It commences (three-four measure) as below :—

is continued (nine-eight measure), with the accompaniment in triplets of quavers ; then in semiquavers ; then (three-four measure) in demisemiquavers :—

and then with the subjoined elaborate contrivance :—

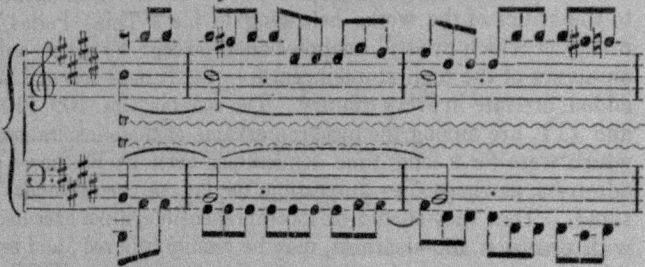

After four bars of this the melody is suddenly interrupted by a discord—introducing an episode, in the shape of a brilliant series of arpeggios for the right hand, upon a dominant *pedal*, the left hand having to sustain a prolonged shake to the point at which the episode in turn gives way to the second section of the theme :—

The ample development of the foregoing now leads—through a gradual *diminuendo*—to a repetition of the melody as it first appeared :—

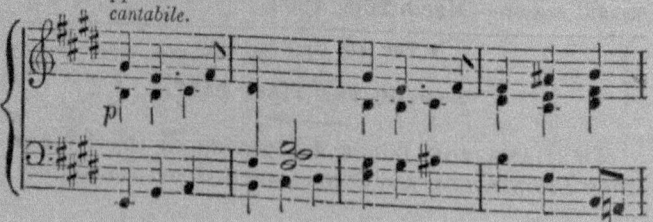

The theme being delivered throughout, *notatim* (minus the "repeats"), the movement closes in an unaffectedly tranquil and expressive manner. This sonata is one of the composer's most aptly designated "tone-poems." The theme of the last movement has never been excelled in tender grace, even by Beethoven. More is the pity that it should so severely tax the mechanical resources of the player.

When some not very profound critic ventured to charge with obscurity certain passages in the second part of Goethe's *Faust*—"Are you quite sure, sir," inquired the poet-philosopher—"that there is nothing the matter with your light?" Such might have been the fair retort of Beethoven in answer to the critics of the works belonging to his "Third Period," many of which are still unappreciated, except by artists and amateurs of the highest intelligence—who, it need scarcely be added, are rare in every country. The sonatas, Ops. 109, 110, and 111, are among the most remarkable of those inspirations which were for a long time condemned even by Beethoven's admirers, as rhapsodies, impossible to play. or even to understand. That they should be incomprehensible, if not executed with precision and clearness, may be readily believed; and as, till of late years, pianists were chiefly occupied in composing and performing fantasias on popular operas, or airs with variations of the same stamp, there was little chance of these deep and poetical works being heard to advantage. The modern "Virtuoso," even of a "classical" turn, was satisfied with a fugue or two by Bach, a concerto and a couple of sonatas by Beethoven, Weber's *Concert Stück*, and Hummel's Septet—as stock in trade, to be served out occasionally to the English public. And so Beethoven had composed the largest number of his pianoforte works for the shelf! Things have changed, however; and the maxim of a distinguished German essayist[*]—"It is for the artist of the highest import—it is, indeed, an absolute necessity, to obtain a complete and perfect performance of whatever Beethoven has written"—seems to be gradually winning acceptance.

The Sonata in E major, Op. 109, was first introduced by Madame Arabella Goddard, at the sixteenth concert of the second season—March 26th, 1860.

---

[*] The late Herr Rellstab.

END OF THE FIRST PART.

Dr. HANS VON BÜLOW will perform on one of Messrs. JOHN BROADWOOD and SONS' Concert Grand Pianofortes.

Entr' Acte.

A LETTER FROM CLEMENTI.

The following letter from Muzio Clementi, the renowned pianist and composer, addressed to the late chief of the eminent house of Collard (then Clementi and Collard), followed as it is by valuable notes on some men of the time, from the pen of Dr. Ferdinand Rahles, will be read with interest by every amateur :—

"DEAR COLLARD,—A happy new year and many returns to all my dear partners and their families! I am on the point of leaving this place for a three weeks' excursion to Naples, but could not think of doing so without acknowledging the receipt of the £500 you sent me; the £150 in notes I received at Berlin, and the rest was forwarded to me at Munich, and I ought no doubt, as a man of business, to have given you notice of it; but when you consider that I am a composer, and a travelling one, and with a young wife too, and, besides, in such a country as Italy, I hope your indulgence will step forward and plead my cause. From this l—— place you will be disappointed if you expect any orders for instruments; but from Naples I shall doubtless have quite a different story to tell. Be prepared then for (I give you timely notice, you see) a grand order, for a small square instrument, which may, perhaps, procure orders for a couple more in twenty or thirty years' time. Don't mistake the matter, though, and imagine the order to be already given; 'tis but a conjecture. Some day or other, however, I shall make ample amends for all this; for, in case the war continues to shut up the passage from Calais to Dover, it is my intention to pay a visit to Moscow, and then, of course, a deluge of orders will ensue, till, at last, your poor delicate fingers will ache with booking and receiving money. Poor Collard! Don't direct your answer here, for, at my return from Naples, I don't know how long I shall favour Rome with my presence, my charming Caroline being in a thriving way, and very unwilling to become the mother of a modern Roman. Direct, therefore, at once, to Leipzig, chez Messrs. Breitkopf and Haertel,* where we shall stay two or three days on our way to Berlin. You need not write immediately to Leipzig, for I should wish to receive your latest intelligence, and we shall not reach that place before the end of March or the beginning of April.

"Has Haertel sent you Haydn's two songs and his sonata? He told me he expected from Beethoven three sonatas for the pianoforte, and a Sinfonia Concertante for pianoforte, violin, and

---

* Breitkopf and Haertel, music publishers at Leipzig.

violoncello, which he will send you, and our share of the price is £50 sterling. Haertel and I had a long conversation upon the subject of Duport,* and we agreed it would not do. In the first place, his name is a little antiquated, which, in musical matters especially, you know, is a great drawback, and the price Haertel found exorbitant. He is sure Romberg will write such a book for 100 louis d'or. What a difference in price and reputation! for he is now esteemed as the first man of his instrument. Have you seen Woelfl's three sontas, Op. 19, dedicated to me? They are published at Erard's. They write to my wife from Hamburg that Lütger and others (Dumark seems to be one of the others, but the name is badly written) sell a great many grand pianofortes under the name of Muzio Clementi, London, and that Lütger, having a workman from our shops, makes small ones in imitation of our patent. Can't you put a stop to that which is wrong in all this, or have you sent to Lütger and others instruments? Have you heard from the Bureau des Arts? I just now learn that Lauska's† instrument has arrived at Stettin, as well as the square one for Mr. Schmuker. From Zurich, Naegeli‡ writes that you have received manuscripts of Beethoven and Woelfl, but he has not received the manuscripts of Cramer and Dussek which you had promised. He expects Woelfl soon, and probably Beethoven will pay him a visit in the course of the winter. Hopes to get MSS. from both, and wishes to know beforehand what manuscripts you could give him as an equivalent. He has sent you patterns of belly-wood, which you have not yet acknowledged. This intelligence is, however, stale, for he sent it me first to Berlin, dated 3rd October. I have agreed to sell him (for the Continent) three new sonatas, which are almost finished, and which I shall send you in good time to print in London. This has nothing to do with the MS. exchange. Now I must beg the favour of you to send me an excellent grand pianoforte for my own use (and which may prove a bait), directed thus:—Monsieur Muzio Clementi, Compositeur de Musique, No. 14, Propstgasse, Berlin. If the port of Hamburg be not open, send it by Stettin, as usual. You may forward it as soon as you like, as my father-in-law will take care of it till my arrival, and I should not like to be in Berlin without such an instrument. A million of compliments to all enquiring friends. My rib wishes me to say a thousand kind things to my partners' good ladies; and I beg to be remembered to Nabob-Banger, Stirring-Hyde, and Puffing Davis. Remaining &c., &c., &c.,

"*Rome, January 1st,* 1805.   "MUZIO CLEMENTI.

"P.S.—Have you sent a grand pianoforte to a pupil of mine of the name of Klengel? 'Twas to have been sent to Berlin."

From the above letter we find that the great Clementi, the Father of the Sonata, was also gifted with remarkable mercantile abilities, and sound judgment in business matters. He seems to

---

* Duport and Bernard Romberg were both celebrated artists on the violoncello, and also composers. The object was a book of instruction for the violoncello.

† Lauska—an excellent pianoforte player and composer, living at Berlin.

‡ Naegeli—music-publisher and composer, at Zurich, also celebrated through his criticisms and literature on music.

have had more propensity for making money than a great artist should incline to; but, nevertheless, he never forgot the artist in favour of the merchant. It is astonishing how many musical revolutions he witnessed during his artistical career of nearly fifty years. He was born in 1752, a time when Handel was still alive, and at the demise of Clementi, 1832, Beethoven and Carl Maria von Weber had both already rested some years in their graves. When Clementi made his appearance in public as an artist, Mozart was only fourteen years of age, Haydn known only in a small limited circle, and at Clementi's death Mendelssohn's first book of "Songs without Words" was just published, and his overture to the *Midsummer Night's Dream* was enjoyed by the musical world about five years. The particularity of having lived through nearly the whole of the newest history of music is observable in his works, especially with regard to technicality, notwithstanding that the beauties in them remained still in their ideality. We find in our musical records that, only from the middle of the past century, artists and composers combined, and entered into branches of their own art in a business-like way, either as musicsellers, music-publishers, or manufacturers of instruments. Before that period they seem to have devoted themselves exclusively to their chosen art, and were only inspired by the divinity of their calling and higher destiny as artists.

As soon as music spread her wings more over the public at large, and fascinated our amateurs, printed and engraved music and instruments came more in demand, and gave proofs that these subjects realized handsome incomes, naturally musicians thought the pitiable share they received from their popularity, either as composers or performers of their works, was not sufficient, and they liked to realize more for themselves by adding a business branch to their art. Handel, one day dissatisfied with his publisher, said to him: "The next time, you compose and I will publish." From Clementi's letter we learn, also, the way in which publishers exchanged their manuscripts, but it seems now, at the present time, different. For enumeration we will mention a few artists who followed Clementi, by combining art and mercantile enterprise together, and with benefit.

IGNACE PLEYEL, a pupil of Haydn, to gain profit from the approbation of his name and the admiration of his popular compositions, established himself as music-publisher at Paris. His business was considered, in a short time, to be the first in Paris, and he realized a handsome fortune. Later, he erected, with the great artist, Kalkbrenner, a pianoforte manufactory, which his son, Camille Pleyel, continued, and the firm is still in existence.

FRANCIS ANTON HOFFMEISTER, a contemporary of Pleyel, and a composer of repute, entered in partnership with the well-known organist, Kuhnel, at Leipzig, as music-publishers. The name of the establishment was the "Bureau de Music." They published not only their own works, but also high class compositions of the best masters. Both commenced as artists and ended as merchants.

NICHOLAS SIMROCK was a celebrated performer on the French horn, in the band of the Prince Elector, at Bonn. When the French entered the Electorate, the Prince dissolved the establishment. Simrock turned an engraver of music, and then added a publishing business, which he extended on a grand scale, and died a rich man.

One of his sons is now the sole proprietor, and the musical world has been enriched by many great and highly noted musical works of their publishing.

HENRY HERZ, the great performer and composer of numerous compositions for the piano, was everywhere known. Besides his artistic pursuits, he established a manufactory of pianos, and the speculation of building a large concert-hall, called "Salle de Herz," at Paris, turned out a very profitable one.

THALBERG was *impresario* of an Italian Opera in the United States at the time of the outbreak of the civil war, and was obliged to dissolve the company. Instead of gain, he lost considerably. And many more may not have been so lucky as some we have mentioned by turning to be merchants and artists together. A reverse case to those we have been enumerating, and which we believe is almost unexampled, is the fact that the celebrated composer, Auber, changed his vocation as a merchant, and became an artist. DR. FERDINAND RAHLES.

Malvern House, Grove Street Road, South Hackney, August, 1874.

Dr. Ferdinand Rahles has overlooked Johann Ludwig Dussek, who, as a music-publisher, in partnership with Corri, failed in this country.—*Musical World.*

———

A LETTER FROM BELLINI ABOUT *NORMA.**

MY DEAR UNCLE,—Despite an opposition party, which is formidable because got up by a powerful person and a wealthy person, my *Norma* has done wonders, and more yesterday evening at the second performance than at the first. The *Giornale Offiziale* of Milan reported yesterday that it was a complete failure, because, on the first night, while the just part of the audience applauded, the adverse faction hissed, and because the powerful person in question is master, and can make the paper write as he pleases. The powerful person does so because he is a most bitter enemy of Pasta, and the rich one because he is a lover of P——, and therefore my enemy.† yesterday evening, however, the opera was even better liked than on the first occasion, the theatre being crammed, the true sign of success; and it was the opera alone which attracted such a crowd, as the two ballads had turned out horrible failures.

On the first night a deep impression was produced by the introduction, Pollio's first air, and Pasta's; the duet between

———

* This "confidential autobiographic account" of the second performance of *Norma* is taken from *I Lunedì d'un Dilettante.*

† We say "he" in speaking both of the "powerful person" and the "rich person," because we suppose that both were men, but we cannot be quite sure. The Italian original runs as follows: " . . . un partito formidabile, a me contrario, perchè suscitato da una persona potente e da una ricchissima . . . e perchè la persona potente è padrona, e può ordinare che il giornale scriva come ad essa piace. La persona potente fa questo, perchè è nemico acerrima della Pasta, e la ricca perchè è l'amante di P . . ., e quindi mia nemica."—TRANSLATOR.

Pollio and Adalgisa did not please, and never will, for it does not please even me; the duet commencing the final trio pleased greatly, but the trio, not being well executed by the singers, because they were tired (having in the morning rehearsed all the second act, etc.) was not well received; for this reason the first act finished without anyone's being applauded and called out. In the second act, with the exception of a chorus which, though successful, did not please very much, everything proved so extraordinarily effective that the opposition was thoroughly overthrown, and incapable of in any way recovering from the blow. I was obliged to appear on the stage as many as four times, alone and with the singers.

Yesterday evening, when the singers gave the trio better, I was called on also for the first act, while the second was more successful than it had been the first night, so that my triumph was decided, and people absolutely hope that the opera which will close the Carnival will be the persecuted *Norma*.

Pasta is divine; let this expression suffice for you to form an idea how she performs her part vocally and dramatically; Donzelli does very well, and sings extremely well, but as yet does not know much of his part; Giulietta Grisi, as Adalgisa, though naturally rather cold, gets on pretty well; the choruses are extraordinarily good.

The public greets the journalist with imprecations, my friends dance with joy; I am most satisfied and doubly contented, because I have vanquished so many of my vile and powerful enemies.

Next week I shall perhaps leave Milan and proceed to Naples, whence, as soon as the weather is milder, I shall start to embrace all my family, relations, and friends. I will then forward you same pieces from *Norma* directly they are printed in Milan.

My health is good, though I am rather exhausted. I will write and inform you how the opera goes on the other evenings. Give all this news to my family, friends, and relations, but do not let anyone read the letter, since it is not very delicate for me to sound my own praises. I embrace you, and trust to retain your goodwill. Your most affectionate   VINCENZO.

Milan, 28th December, 1831.

Sig. Vincenzo Ferliti—Catania.

Part II.

SONATA, in A major, Op. 69, for Pianoforte and Violoncello. *Beethoven.*

(Ninth performance at the Popular Concerts.)

Allegro ma non tanto—A major.
Scherzo, allegro molto—A minor; with Trio—A major.
Adagio cantabile—E major; leading to
Allegro vivace—A major.

Dr. HANS VON BÜLOW and Signor PEZZE.

This sonata, the most celebrated of the five composed by Beethoven for pianoforte and violoncello, was first published by Breitkopf and Härtel, in April, 1809. It is dedicated to the Baron von Gleichenstein. In Professor Schneller's *Lebensumriss*—Vol. 1 of his Posthumous works—we read the following remarks on Beethoven:

"In life he was cheerful and *spirituel* (*geistrich*), straightforward, and simple, but often enveloped in the profound sentimental feeling of melancholy peculiar to poetic minds. It was in such a state of mind that, on the sonata dedicated to his friend Baron Ignatius von Gleichenstein, he wrote '*Inter Lacrimas et Luctum.*'"

Allegro ma non tanto (first theme).

(Episode, in A minor.)

(Second subject, in E major.)

Violoncello.

Cello.

Scherzo.

Trio.

(Introduction to the last movement.)

Finale (first theme).

(Second theme.)

(Peroration to second theme.)

The Sonata in A major was first introduced by Mr. Charles Hallé and Signor Piatti, at the twenty-fifth concert of the second season—June 18, 1860.

NEW SONG, Miss ANTOINETTE STERLING.

Music by Arthur Sullivan.

Words by ADELAIDE PROCTOR.

"THOU ART WEARY."

Hush! I cannot bear to see thee
  Stretch thy tiny hands in vain;
Dear, I have no bread to give thee—
  Nothing, child, to ease thy pain.
When God sent thee first to bless me,
  Proud and thankful too was I;
Now, my darling, I—thy mother—
  Almost long to see thee die.
Sleep, my darling, thou art weary;
God is good, but life is dreary.

Better thou shouldst perish early,
  Starve so soon, my darling one,
Than in helpless sin and sorrow
  Vainly live—as I have done!
Better that thy angel spirit
  With my joy, my peace were flown,
Than thy heart grow cold and careless,
  Reckless, hopeless—like my own!
Sleep, my darling, thou art weary;
God is good, but life is dreary.

I am wasted, dear, with hunger,
  And my brain is all opprest;
I have scarcely strength to press thee,
  Wan and feeble, to my breast.
Patience, baby, God will help us:
  Death will come to thee and me;
He will take us to his Heaven,
  Where no want or pain can be.
Sleep, my darling, thou art weary;
God is good, but life is dreary.

---

* Published by CHAPPELL and Co. 50, New Bond Street.

—————

AN INTERVAL OF FIVE MINUTES.

—————

TRIO, in B flat major, Op. 52, for Pianoforte, Violin, and Violoncello. *Anton Rubinstein.*

(Second performance at the Popular Concerts.)

Allegro—B flat major.
Adagio—D minor.
Presto (scherzo)—F major; with meno mosso
(trio)—C major.
Allegro appassionato—B flat major.

Dr. HANS VON BÜLOW, M. SAINTON, and Signor PEZZE.

Allegro (leading theme).

Out of the various component parts of this theme, allowing for the *cantabile* phrase, with its tributaries, which constitutes what is understood as the "second subject"—the whole *allegro* may be said to be constructed—with a unity of purpose commented upon in a recent analysis of a trio by Joachim Raff, who, like M. Rubinstein, is one of Schumann's most eminent followers. Immediately after the first full close in the tonic (B flat), we find the theme developed in a fragmentary way, as below :—

Violin and Cello in octaves.

It will be observed that the first half of the first section of the theme is separated by two crotchet rests from the other, besides beginning on the last, instead of the first half of the bar. The second theme is ushered in by a sort of prologue, which must speak for itself. The melody proper is as subjoined :—

Violin.

Part of the pianoforte accompaniment is omitted in the foregoing example ; but, consisting, as it does, simply of triplet *arpeggios* for the right hand, it is unnecessary to cite it.

After the second theme has been fully developed, the peroration of the first section of the movement begins with a new treatment, in the imitative style, of a feature in the leading theme (✳), which will at once be recognised by attentive hearers :—

The pianoforte, as will be observed, accompanies this with brilliant passages of divided chords, in triplets. The second part is almost wholly devoted to more or less elaborate developments of the first theme, and the various forms under which it has already appeared. It commences as below, with the theme in a new key :—

We have then an episode, in which the first theme (again in a new key), in "augmentation"—every crotchet now becoming a minim, and every quaver a crotchet—appears in the bass :—

(Episode.)

Leading theme augmented.

Further, yet once more in a new key, the theme again appears as a bass, in double augmentation, what were first crotchets, and subsequently minims, now assuming the dimensions of semibreves :—

(Pianoforte part only.)

Leading theme in double augmentation.

In the foregoing example the stringed instruments sustain chords in full harmony, which it is not necessary to quote. Nor are further citations from the first movement called for. The leading theme returns, in B flat, the primary key, and, allowing for the usual changes of tonality, every passage that has been quoted, with certain unimportant modifications, is heard again. The *coda*, exclusively built upon the leading subject, will speak for itself.

A brief extract from the principal theme and episodes of the *adagio* must suffice :—

Adagio (leading theme).

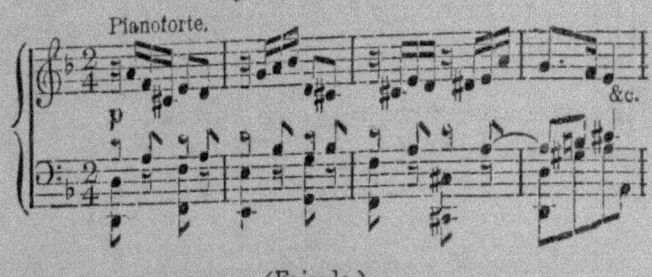

(Episode.)

The second theme proper appears in B flat :—

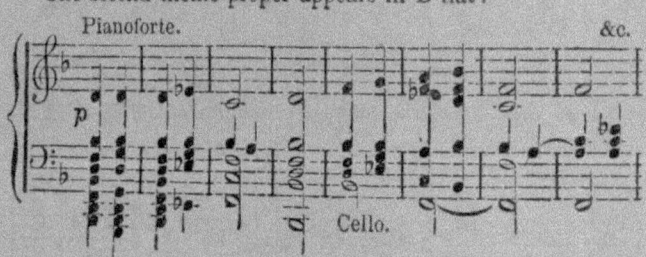

It then modulates to the orthodox dominant, and appears in F, *forte* :—

(Second theme—string parts only.)

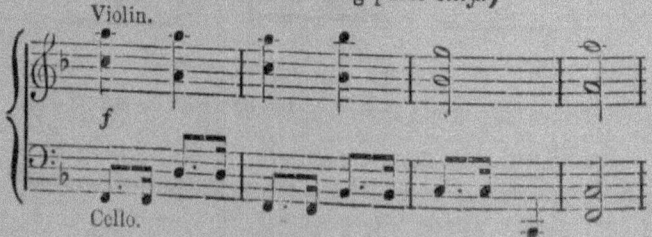

The pianoforte plays a bustling accompaniment, in demi-semiquaver *arpeggios*, which need not be cited. The leading theme then comes back in quite a new form. The violin gives the melody, and the violoncello the bass, "*pizzicato*," as below :—

—while the pianoforte plays an independent part after the subjoined pattern :—

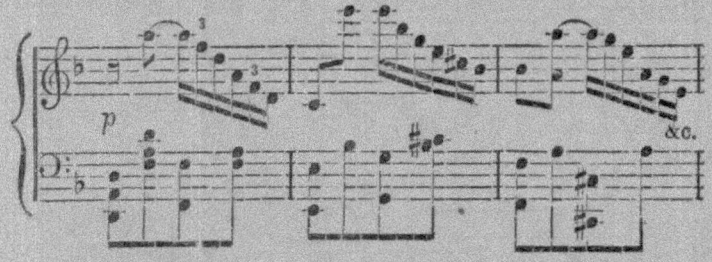

Further quotations from this *adagio* would be superfluous.

A short extract from the *scherzo* (*presto*) and its companion *trio* will answer all purposes, as the entire movement is for the most part in the customary form.

E

Scherzo (F major).

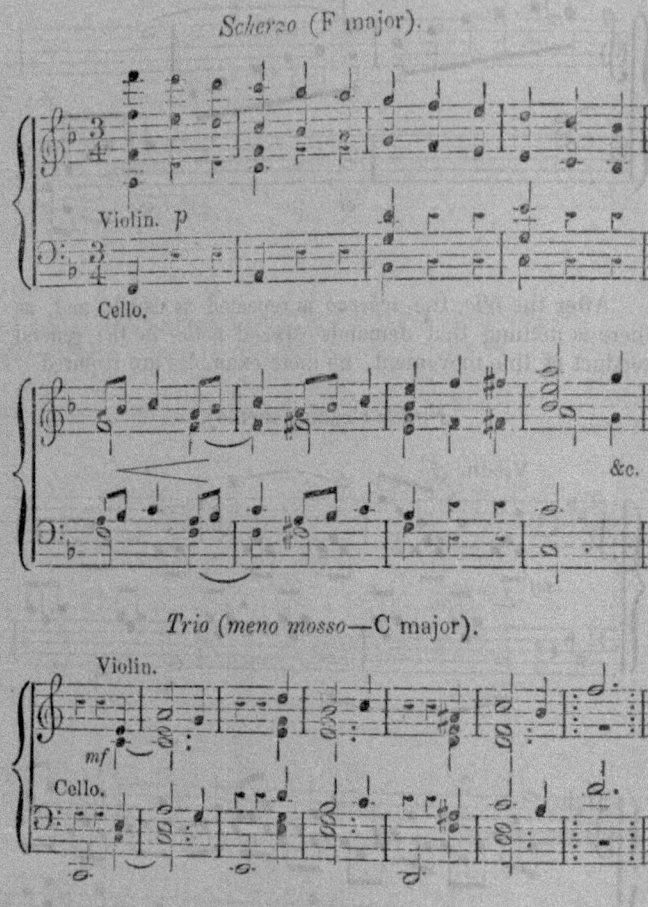

Trio (meno mosso—C major).

The pianoforte then proceeds as follows, accompanied by holding notes for the leading instruments:—

After the *trio*, the *scherzo* is repeated as usual; and, as there is nothing that demands especial notice in the general conduct of the movement, no more examples are required.

Finale (leading theme).

44

(Tributary.)

(Episode—G minor.)

Violin.

(Second theme—F major.)

Violin. Reference to 1st theme.

Cello.

Violin.

Cello.

The violin then takes up the melody, accompanied by the violoncello, with an *arpeggio* for the pianoforte.

(Tributary to second theme.)

Before the return of the leading theme, we have a remarkable episode, a few bars of which must suffice to indicate the character :—

&c.

It will be observed that fragments of the principal subject are occasionally mixed up with this episode. After the theme once more appears, in the primary key (B flat), the movement is conducted to an end, with few and unimportant modifications.

Anton Rubinstein was born at Wechwotynez, a village in Moldavia, on the 30th November, 1829. He was taught the elements of pianoforte playing by his mother, herself an adept, and made such rapid progress as to induce his parents to place him under the care of Villoing, then chief professor of the instrument at Moscow. Villoing was Rubinstein's only master for the pianoforte. His visits to this country, since the first—in 1843, when Ernst, Charles Hallé, Léopold de Meyer, and that remarkable prodigy, Charles Filtsch, came first among us (the year before the arrival of Sainton and Joseph Joachim)—have been frequent, and invariably redounded to his fame.

The Trio in B flat was first introduced by Dr. Hans von Bülow, M. Sainton, and Signor Piatti, at the eighteenth concert of the sixteenth season—February 2, 1874.

END OF THE FOUR HUNDRED AND EIGHTY-SIXTH CONCERT.

J. MALLETT, PRINTER, 59, WARDOUR STREET, SOHO. W.

SATURDAY POPULAR CONCERTS.

SATURDAY AFTERNOON, NOV. 14th, 1874.

QUARTET, in G major, Op. 54, No. 2, for two Violins,
Viola, and Violoncello. ....*Haydn*.

(First time at the Popular Concerts.)

MM. SAINTON, L. RIES, ZERBINI, and PEZZE.

LIEDER, { " Der Tod und das Mädchen." ....*Schubert*.
{ " O Jugend, o schöne Rosenzeit." .... *Mendelssohn*.

Miss ANTOINETTE STERLING.

CONCERTO, in the Italian style, for Pianoforte alone...........*Bach*.

Dr. HANS VON BÜLOW.

INTRODUCTION and **POLONAISE BRILLANTE**, for
Pianoforte and Violoncello ....*Chopin*.

Dr. HANS VON BÜLOW and Signor PEZZE.

NEW SONG, " Thou art weary." ....*Arthur Sullivan*.

Miss ANTOINETTE STERLING.

QUINTET, in D minor, Op. 130, for Pianoforte, two Violins,
Viola, and Violoncello .... *Spohr*.

(First time at the Popular Concerts.)

MM. HANS VON BÜLOW, SAINTON, L. RIES.
ZERBINI, and PEZZE.

Conductor - Sir JULIUS BENEDICT.

I

www.ingramcontent.com/pod-product-compliance
Lightning Source LLC
Chambersburg PA
CBHW081215170626
46811CB00010B/3307